December, 1997

Dear William,

merry christmas!
We hope you enjoy this
cincinnati classic— Its
Brendan's favorite. We live
about 5 miles from
Sardinia concrete and see
their trucks daily. We're
still looking for slim in
old number 44.

We Love you + miss you.
Uncle Pat, Aunt Patty,
Colleen, Brendan + Danny

THE NEIGHBORHOOD TRUCKER

by Louise Borden

illustrated by Sandra Speidel

SCHOLASTIC
HARDCOVER

SCHOLASTIC INC.
New York

Special thanks to Jim, Charlie, and Slim
for their many kindnesses.

— L. B.

Library of Congress Cataloging-in-Publication Data

Borden, Louise.
  The neighborhood trucker / by Louise Borden; illustrated by
Sandra Speidel.
    p. cm.
Summary: Fascinated by trucks and wanting to be a trucker,
Elliot looks at all kinds of trucks and emulates Slim, his favorite
trucker.
  ISBN 0-590-42584-6
[1. Trucks—Fiction. 2. Truck driving—Fiction.] I. Speidel, Sandra,
ill. II. Title.
PZ7.B64827Ne   1990
[E]—dc19   89-6225
                                                              CIP
                                                               AC

12 11 10 9 8 7 6 5 4 3 2   1 2 3 4/9

Book design by Laurie McBarnette

Printed in the U.S.A.   36
First Scholastic printing, September 1990

For Ted, who has always known
what he wants to become,
and for his father, who understands why.
— L. B.

To Ryan and Zoe.
— S. S.

While the neighborhood was playing
with cars and blocks and doll buggies,
Elliot Long was becoming a trucker.

Elliot lived
just down the road
from Sardinia Concrete.
Every day
he watched
the Sardinia trucks
rumble past his house
to their morning jobs.
The huge white drums turned slowly
round and round and round again,
spinning the bright red letters
SARDINIA
for all to see.

And in the late afternoon,
Elliot watched the big, loud trucks
rumble past him on the highway toward home.
Shiny blue cabs and
round rolling wheels of silver,
covered with the dust of the day's work.

On Sundays Elliot and his father
stood in the Sardinia yard
and counted the trucks
in their long, silent rows.

Number 44 was Elliot's favorite.
Its driver was named Slim.
Slim wore a Sardinia cap and tall, dusty boots,
and on his jacket were two faded patches.
One said, "Slim."
One said, "Sardinia Concrete."

So while the neighborhood was selling lemonade and
drawing dinosaurs and chasing squirrels in the park,
Elliot Long was becoming a trucker.
"Call me Slim," he said.

Every day Elliot stopped to watch
foundations being poured
and sidewalks being repaired.
Elliot watched dump trucks dump gravel
and flatbeds haul pipes.
Elliot watched garbage trucks up the street
and moving vans down the street.

Elliot watched cherry pickers
and gasoline tankers
and bulldozers in the mud.

Each truck was its own shape
and color and sound
when Elliot was watching.
And he was watching a lot.

Elliot watched the big rigs on the interstate.
Flashing past. Always in a hurry.
KENWORTH MACK FREIGHTLINER AUTOCAR MARMON FORD
GMC PETERBILT INTERNATIONAL WHITE OSHKOSH
DIAMOND REO MERCEDES WESTERN STAR and BROCKWAY.

Some were from Utah and Nevada and New York.
Some were from Missouri and Massachusetts and Maine.
Some drivers yelled, "Hi!" and pulled on their horns.
Some tipped their caps and called, "See ya, Sonny!"
Some stared down, silent and tired.
Each trucker had a name and a home far away.
Each trucker was his own special self
when Elliot Long was watching.
And he was watching a lot.

Elliot watched fire trucks roaring to a fire.
He watched cranes
and tow trucks
and eighteen-wheelers
in city traffic.
He listened to their horns
and he listened to their brakes.

In winter, while the neighborhood
was rolling snowballs and pulling sleds
and skating on the pond,
Elliot Long was plowing the driveway.

In summer, while the neighborhood
was playing tag and scoring goals
and hitting home runs,
Elliot Long was grading the field.

Elliot's neighbor Polly
liked ballerinas and balloons.
Elliot's neighbor Josh
liked rockets and cupcakes and books.
Elliot's neighbor Frances
liked mudpies and frogs and fish.
Elliot's brother Rob
played goalie and third base.
And Elliot Long liked trucks.
"Call me Slim," said Elliot.

On his birthday
Elliot took the neighborhood
to the Sardinia yard.

They all got new Sardinia caps,
and Elliot, well, he was waiting for a ride.
"Number 44, please," said Elliot.

It was late afternoon,
and the neighborhood watched
for the shiny blue cabs
and round rolling wheels of silver,
covered with the dust of the day's work.

In came Number 18.
And right behind was Number 23.
And a little later came Number 51.
But no Number 44.

"Maybe he's gone to the ballet," said Polly.
"Maybe he's gone to the moon," said Josh.
"Maybe he's just off fishing," said Frances.
"Maybe he's catching a game," said Rob.

But Elliot Long
shook his head
and kept his hand
ready in his pocket,
ready to wave to Slim.

And while the neighborhood was eating cake
and touching mud flaps
and mixing gravel and cement,
Elliot Long was watching for Slim.

And then down the highway
with rumbles of dust,
sure enough,
there came Slim,
driving Number 44.

The huge, white drum turned slowly
round and round and round again,
and Elliot had a slow, wide smile
for all to see.

"How about a ride?" said Slim.
In the palm of his hand
were the patches from his jacket.
The one that said, "Slim."
And the one that said, "Sardinia Concrete."
And while the neighborhood was becoming ballerinas
and clowns and astronauts and cooks and
librarians and mudpie makers and froggers and
fishermen and skaters and goalies and third basemen...

Elliot Long was already a trucker.
"Call me Slim."